WOMBATS CAN'T FLY

WOMBATS CAN'T

Michael Dugan   Jane Burrell

FLY

RANDOM HOUSE AUSTRALIA

The young wombats found
something bright and shiny
caught in a bush.

They hid it and ran
back to their burrow.

'We're going flying,'
they told their mother.
'Don't be silly,' she replied.
'Wombats can't fly.
Wombats can chew roots
with their strong teeth.'

The young wombats
went exploring to the tip.
They found an old
shopping basket.

They dragged it back to their burrow and hid it under a bed.

'We're going flying,'
they told their father.

'Don't be silly,'
he replied.
'Wombats can't fly.
Wombats can dig burrows
with their strong claws.'

The young wombats
found a long piece
of string that had
fallen from a kite.

They rolled it up carefully
and hid it in a gumboot.

'We're going flying,'
they told their grandmother.
'Don't be silly,' she replied,
'Wombats can't fly. Wombats can find
their way through the bush on dark
moonless nights.'

The young wombats took
the basket and string
to a clearing near their burrow.

They fetched their treasure
from its hiding place.

'We're going flying,'
they told their grandfather.
'Don't be silly,' he yawned.
'Wombats can't fly.'

'Wombats can sleep snugly
through the cold days
of winter.'

The young wombats climbed
into their basket.

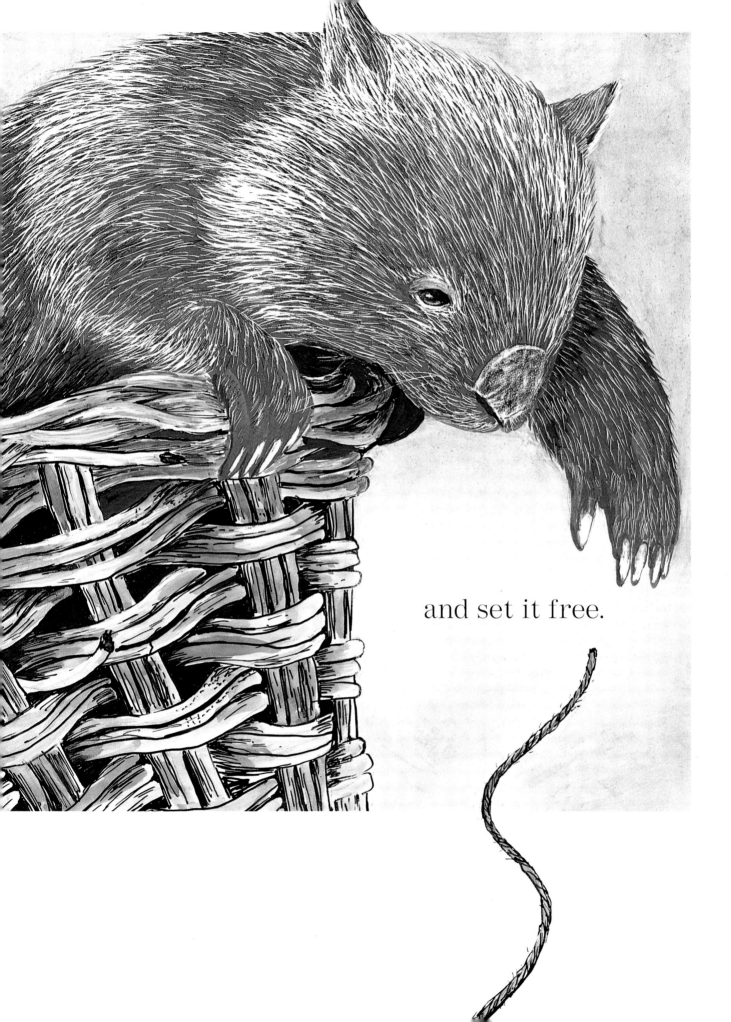

and set it free.

It rose gently into the air.
'Look at us,' they called.

'Come back! Come back!'
cried their mother,
their father,
their grandmother
and their grandfather.

'We're going flying,'
the young wombats
called back as they
soared above the trees.

For my sister, Sally Dugan. *MD*

For Lloyd, Inga and Ellen,
with love. *JB*

Random House Australia Pty Ltd
Level 3, 100 Pacific Highway, North Sydney NSW 2060
http://www.randomhouse.com.au

Sydney   New York   Toronto
London   Auckland   Johannesburg

First published by Random House Australia in 1996
Paperback edition first published by Random House Australia in 2006
Text copyright © Michael Dugan 1996
Illustrations copyright © Jane Burrell 1996

National Library of Australia
Cataloguing-in-Publication Entry

Dugan, Michael, 1947–.
Wombats can't fly.

ISBN 0091827698 (hbk).
ISBN 0091829380 (pbk).

1. Wombats – Juvenile fiction. I. Burrell, Jane, 1951–.
II. Title.

A823.3

Typeset by Asset Typesetting Pty Ltd, Sydney.
Manufactured in Hong Kong, Sing Cheong Printing Co. Ltd
Production by Vantage Graphics, Sydney.

10 9 8 7 6 5 4 3